C000093453

me
in search of
you

me
in search of
you

We popped. We texted. We swirled.
I promise there's more to it.

Jenna Langbaum

Andrews McMeel
PUBLISHING®

Andrews McMeel Publishing
a division of Andrews McMeel Universal
1130 Walnut Street, Kansas City, Missouri 64106

www.andrewsmcmeel.com

21 22 23 24 25 VEP 10 9 8 7 6 5 4 3 2 1

ISBN: 978-1-5248-6249-7

Library of Congress Control Number: 2020951033

Editor: Patty Rice
Designer: Sierra S. Stanton
Production Editor: Elizabeth A. Garcia
Production Manager: Carol Coe

To all the mes in search of yous—
we're on this island together.

Part 1

We **POPPED**

There was so much time in the car parked outside a
pizza dumpster. There was gravel, tight wool over wool,
and cheeks so red they could burn off. There were piña
coladas at Chili's and a pink cowboy hat you gave me
before graduation. There was a time when I found your
Crocs endearing and you found my singing in public
charming. We weren't meant to stretch across the country,
but we tried and ripped apart. Even so, the root of our
love was kidlike and simple—an arm-in-arm, come-sit-
next-to-me kind of thing; it dizzies me now.

I'm sorry I gave you the ending. But I promise there's more to it.

We **LATCHED**

I bought you an avocado, put a Post-it on it, and drove away. We kissed for the first time that night, illuminated under a Subway sandwich sign. I was lava, and you were ice. You—quiet, sewn to your bicycle, methodically explaining the clouds, the dirt, the way alcohol slows your brain. And me—loud, feverishly writing, always on the brink of a monologue about the clouds, my heart, the way alcohol sparks us. You showed me how to be calm and allow someone to enter. I showed you how to write a birthday card and rub someone's back. And for those things, we will always have weight.

I tried to ride your bike, and I fell, and we both felt bad. I had no business on a bicycle, and you had no business with me.

We **CRYSTALLIZED**

I cut your hair over the sink, and we belly laughed. It is this laugh that fluttered through the hallowed halls of my rib cage. *You did a horrible job,* you said in the bathroom mirror, throwing toothpaste at my cheek. I lived in this ancient apartment—with every step came a thousand creaks, a thousand mothballs. We lived in this ancient way—with all the time in the world, the only explorers seemingly left on this snowy island. Today, the wooden apartment is empty, floors still soaked with garlic from the pizza place below, standing as a monument of memories and thick, gray dust.

Somehow, I fucked up a buzzcut.

We **FUSED**

The first time I was certain about you, we were in the car, your silver Subaru unraveling the spool of gray central New York, snow tapping at the windows. *How great is it that we are together?* You said it so sincerely, your brown eyes broke out in a panic. *Almost as great as my new haircut.* Your awkward rebuttal was like salt over the saccharine sentiment you leaked. I smiled so widely, my lips wobbled. *Both are.* We drove for miles and miles, and it was sacred—the snow, the sweetness, the morning stretching ever so softly into languid afternoon.

It's hard to write about happy things.

We **SHINED**

We said *I love you* in December while we were brushing
our teeth—it had been only a few months—I was in wool
socks and that Christmas sweater that scratched us both.
I almost said it in the parking lot next to the dumpster
the Monday before, but you put your hand over my
mouth. *Is the bathroom any better? Yes, cleaner,*
you said and smirked.

*Right after, we went to Dunkin' Donuts and sat there all day eating
powdered doughnuts and smiling.*

We **WON**

On my birthday you made me frozen chicken wings we bought at the gas station. I braided my hair, and you told me I looked like a cartoon princess. We sat on the couch, and I fell asleep with you on my lap. You were a prize then.

I will always remember the words "cartoon princess."

We **CRACKED**

Should we give it a go? We stared at the creamy spread of
states on Google Maps from New York to Texas. *I feel like
we kind of have to,* you said quietly, and I looked out of your
Subaru knowing I would think about this moment often.

*Before all this, Texas was a T-shirt with a star on it my dad got me
in Dallas while on a business trip.*

We **TIGHTENED**

It was my birthday. *Let me smoosh cake into the phone,* you said, and I grinned. *How's it taste?* It was moments like these that I felt the gap of states between New York and Texas clasp shut; it was moments like these I felt we could make it.

I would often excessively doll myself up to FaceTime—just to try, just to make it feel more than it was.

We **LEAKED**

You wanted me to "get into" camping, to learn how
to be quieter, to stop gallivanting. You wanted me to
be someone else, and I felt the same about you. It was
something we never said out loud except for once—in the
parking lot near the Alamo. *I'm sorry,* we both said shyly
and knotted our hands on the clutch.

*I remember we wore almost the same outfit to the Alamo. We looked
like siblings dressed by Mom.*

We **SLURRED**

On New Year's Eve, we booked a cheap hotel downtown
and spent the day nipping at each other. *Why is it so loud
here?* you squinted. *Why don't you like New York?* I
shrieked. And instead of answering, we watched *Superbad*
with mugs of Jameson. And it helped: once drunk, we were
better—brighter. We laughed wildly. *If only you could act
like this always,* you said, and I sunk. At midnight, we
went to a dive bar and ate chicken fingers. There is a paper
crown I found in the bar that night, and, until recently,
it sat on my nightstand. It's now in a bin in my parents'
basement. It's not you that makes me sad anymore but
rather the commute of the crown, the definitive movement
where our silver moment moved out of focus.

Thank god for McLovin.

I **CRUNCHED**

You're being ridiculous, you know that? you screamed
into the phone. *Wait, please don't,* I said as you hung up.
I was sitting in the hallway, knees up, staring at a yellow
umbrella outside my neighbor's. Our phone calls were
taken outside my apartment in an effort to keep your roars
and my pleading away from my roommates. *Can you come
to New York soon?* I had asked desperately. The snaps were
visceral, like tough, dry wood cracking apart. It was in
these moments on the gray carpet in my hallway I twisted
into a different version of myself—manic, weak, and
crippled. It was these moments on the gray carpet I never
told anyone about.

*My neighbors would scramble inside at the sight of me pacing in
my leopard pj set.*

We **MOURNED**

There was no Valentine's Day that year. I bought you pajamas, and we watched a lot of TV on your Texas futon. You held my stomach when I said it hurt—I often moved your hands to the places I wanted them. We were so far from your college room—mattress on the floor, beer caps on the wall, orange helmet on a hook—and even further from that morning we sat in your car grinning widely. You didn't realize what you were getting yourself into, but you always swore you did.

You forgot about Valentine's Day. You ran to CVS and bought me a condolence card with a lion on it, and I cried.

We **SILENCED**

I wasn't ever sure if we found the same things funny. We fought the loudest when we went camping because you didn't want me to hate it and I so did. I loved the having-beers-and-talking of each of our weekends. I loved the doughnuts and the choosing of the restaurants and the moments of sleep when we were so quiet and so kind to each other.

It's probably a bad sign that I liked you most when you were sleeping.

We **DAMPENED**

The last time we were loving to each other was in a hotel room outside Marfa, just before 2am. The room was damp and vast, the curtains sagged like heavy tears, and the TV's blue steam simmered out like smoke from a cigarette. We were sprawled on the bed, robes half open, chests out like old men. *We are gonna figure it all out,* you said, and the lamplight ached like a spotlight on our two bodies twining together.

We had spent the day on a white water raft with your family, screaming at each other. It felt unfair—you knew I wasn't one for the outdoors.

We **ROTTED**

You were sitting at the bar counter, and I was standing—
another one of your visits to New York. *Be nice,* you
said as your horrible friend Agnes entered the restaurant.
You're the only person who doesn't think I'm nice, my
eyes welled up—I was at a new level of sensitive, even
for me. The night before, we screamed in the hallway of
my apartment until, finally, I whispered, *I am not sure you
love me anymore. No, I just hate New York.* I sipped my
beer, a lifeline to the swelter of June and our dilapidated
presence, my eyes on Agnes. You were nodding and
laughing and gushing over her, and, of course, she was
loving it. I put my hand on your leg, but you shrugged it
off. In two days, you would be back in Texas, and I would
be flailing, replaying this moment over and over.

Don't even get me started on Agnes . . .

We **SUCCUMBED**

Halloween in leather pants, I headed into the stairwell to call you. Your voice was shrill. *I don't think I get your costume,* the whir of San Antonio highway behind you. I picked stucco off of the bannister. *How do you not get it? Everyone knows bad Sandy. Not everyone loves the same things as you.* You hung up abruptly. These are the moments I would label "The End."

I still think everyone knows who bad Sandy is.

I **COLLAPSED**

What is hard to admit or even articulate were the dark bits, the crusted caverns, the stretches of time when my loneliness, your isolation, our depression would be all-encompassing and as large as the state of Texas. I lived in a parade of heaving, soft talking, coddling, big fat tears, brushing your hair through the phone followed startlingly by a groundswell of silence, then shoves and stomps and words that bit and bore into me. *Please stop, stop crying, stop putting pressure, stop making everything such a big deal, OK?* Like a spiked boomerang to the gut, like a grip that twisted and ripped, you ran me red, and you ran me ragged. But what is harder to admit or even articulate is why I let you.

Each day, I forgive a bit more.

I **UNDRESSED**

I drank margaritas with a friend the Monday after
Thanksgiving in the middle of the day. Sharp, cheap
tequila drifting through me at a dive bar outfitted in
polyester mermaids and netting. We laughed loudly with
the pirate bartender. And I saw the beginnings of what I
could be without the dark wool cloak of us sagging on my
back. It was then I decided to unbutton you, take off the
cloak, and shove it in the back of the closet.

*Cowgirl Seahorse is where the new me sputtered her way up out of
the ocean.*

We **CLAMORED**

Outside the Duane Reade on Fulton Street, I called you
back for the final time. Clenching my glassy eyes shut,
we broke into bits of slime and silence and sewage. We
knew we might never see each other again. When I hung
up, I felt enormous. I took a cab to my friend's apartment,
staring out the window with this wild new energy. *You are
on the other side.* Relief and sadness bounced like rockets
under my skin.

*I think about this night a lot. I was a rabid animal, howling and
homely prowling near Duane Reade in the rain.*

We **SWIRLED**

A week after we broke up, you sent me a Mazzy Star song
and said, *There was a heart in here after all. I told you so,*
I wrote back and crawled into my bed with the lights on
and the room spinning around.

You never liked my emo music until I stopped sending it to you.

Part 2

I **FIZZED**

Just two hours after I hung up with a Texas landline, I
found myself clenched on a couch, fingers around the
stem of a wine glass, face glimmering with excessive eye
shadow. You changed your profile picture from us in my
backyard to you alone on your bike—our postmortem
immediate and public. I knew I needed to do the same,
to solve this one element of my complicated new start.
And just like that, I was applying cold compresses to my
swollen face and then a regime of foundation, highlighter,
and blush. *You have to laugh,* my friend said kindly.
And I did. In some ways, I am happy to have the picture.
Although sort of deranged, there is a pinch of hope in my
eyes that's stayed with me.

*My third profile picture—voilà, there she is, the rabid animal all
dolled up.*

I **CAREENED**

I knew there would be time to be retrospective, to stare
out at the water and long for you. I was nowhere near
there. Your name was a bruise I covered with thick
yellow concealer; our relationship was a stench I doused
in flower perfume and silver vodka. I spent my time in
the back of the bar in a tight black dress trying to get
somebody, anybody, to look at me. And there were many
times I would catch a glimpse, the smallest sliver of
myself in the dirty bathroom mirror, and I would wonder
what you would think.

*I repurchased the same haggard black frock from Forever 21 over
and over again.*

We **GAZED**

Look at the moon, you texted me from Texas—one of the final things you asked of me. I looked to the sky coarse with stars and one big, fat yellow face.

I was at my office Christmas party in Times Square sharing sangria with my middle-aged friend Lydia. She smiled sadly.

Jenna Langbaum

I **FROTHED**

I kissed someone I didn't know on New Year's Eve in
a Chinatown warehouse—green lights and a giant gold
balloon falling on our faces. I closed my eyes and let the
moment fizz.

*The next day I ate heaps of chicken parm in calm, peaceful solitude
and relished.*

We **ORBITED**

We met online. My first online date. You said the same
was true for you, but I later learned that wasn't true.
I knew I wasn't ready, but there I was, pacing on the
sidewalk in the bell bottoms I had bought in Austin
just three months earlier. I entered the basement bar;
my stomach was a ball of lava and whiskey. There you
were—engulfed in darkness, holding a beer. I expected a
big reveal, a spotlight to land on you crooning a country
song, but there wasn't even music at the bar, and the
moment grew bigger and longer. I cowered at you, eyes
expanding into dense, white planets. *Hi.* You were unsure
of what to do with me. Eventually, we clunkily embraced.
My chest was shaking. I watched myself in bewilderment
and sat down.

I think I asked what your job was seven separate times.

We **COLLECTED**

Walking me to the subway, the cold biting and bleary, you held my hand. We came across a box of books, and we decided to each take one—I took *The City Beneath Us: Building the New York Subways,* and you took *Huckleberry Finn. Finders keepers,* you said, and we smiled in agreement. The feeling of being wanted like a spinning microwave thawing old, pink meat.

It felt weirdly symbolic of what our dynamic could be. The subway book was probably not the most romantic choice in retrospect.

We **LIQUIFIED**

Our third date, we had calzones at a small Italian restaurant in Park Slope. This was my first third date—ever. I felt your eyes hovering in bemusement on my velvet tank top. I suddenly felt tacky and young. You were going on about a short story you were writing—a beautiful girl gets her tongue stuck on ice and can't speak. *But it must have melted—the ice? No, that's the whole point of the story. What?* I drank heavily and stared at you. There was a feeling that I didn't have much to say. Or rather I didn't know what to say. Or maybe it was that whatever I said didn't seem to matter. I couldn't figure out why you were even there or why I was.

I didn't really want a calzone in this tight, tiny top, but, alas, I was learning the mechanics of how to be my real self on a date.

We **DRIPPED**

I found myself often looking at this picture of you—
the blurry one where you're leaning across the table
at the falling-apart, snow-leaking-from-the-ceiling
Mediterranean restaurant in Utica, New York—and I
would feel the prickly this-feels-like-it-never-happened,
I-forget-the-sound-of-your-voice, I'll-never-have-the-I'll-
go-to-the-car-wash-with-you-rub-your-belly-pick-the-
sleep-sand-from-your-eyes feeling. And the melancholia
would splash and spread.

What do I do with this picture? Do I throw it out? Your rosy cheeks
suddenly stained with yesterday's salad and tuna fish.

We **THAWED**

You made a movie about the deli in your hometown in Massachusetts. It was our seventh date—*You can stop counting,* you said, smiling. The movie was a black-and-white silent film, and it was making me cringe. *Are you liking it?* It was a moment of earnest, the most sincere I'd seen you since we met. I nodded vehemently. *Why aren't you laughing? This part is the best—when Joe throws the turkey in the air.* I giggled along—I didn't know you well enough to tease you. Joe missed the turkey catch, and the whole deli was in uproar, including his love interest parked behind the cashier. This led Joe to duck in shame in the freezer, his head falling to his knees. I was looking at your face in full, uncontrollable laughter, and I wanted to climb in there with Joe.

This is the kind of thing where I would tell my friends (and myself)—"Isn't that amazing? He's so cool." Meanwhile, in the moment, I just KNEW, I knew.

We **HUMIDIFIED**

You were a teacher. Books like weeds crawled up your
shelves and out of your mouth. *You probably haven't read
this,* you said and threw a Junot Díaz book at me. *I read!*
I proclaimed like a first grader finishing *Goodnight Moon.*
You corrected me often, said I was too romantic about
things. *You exaggerate, or maybe you're just young.*
I cried in the moldy bathroom, the yellow light pounding
on my knees, because it all felt foreign, the strangeness
of a stranger, the swirl of a new life I was pasting over
my old one.

*"He was stern" was really the moral of the story. How I would
have hated him as my teacher.*

We **SEARED**

It had been two months of seeing each other, and it was Valentine's Day. *We are so new. I'm sure nothing will happen. Who even knows?* That's what I found myself saying over and over, but the incessant red at the bodega, at the office, on the heads of children, the pedals on the 6 train floor—it started to singe. And when I hadn't heard from you by 9pm, I knew—the light in the hallway of my gut buzzed a blaring, heated red.

I proceeded to have a big bowl of pasta and get wasted.

I **BURROWED**

And so it began—the filth, the grit, the unitchable itch
of knowing suddenly, sublimely, and fully that I would
never hear from you ever again. The anxiety of getting
ghosted is a mountain, and I made the scale—burrowed
into the downtown C train, my blood swirling, my back
a deadweight. I cried like the emo teenager I harbor
inside. I stared at a small baby's hand next to me, and
I longed to hold it.

The soundtrack is always Bon Iver, thick, blaring Bon Iver.

We **BUZZED**

Hey, I'd like to see you—my high school boyfriend groped up from the soil six years later. I was in disbelief, wandering around Macy's debating chenille blankets for my grandma. I stared at the screen, suddenly feeling so young and malleable, knots loosening in my heart, my flip-book of memories soaring. *I just want to be with someone who knows me,* I thought as I sat on a crimson bedspread covered in plastic. *Hi,* I wrote back, and thin snow sputtered outside.

My high school self had a real field day with this phase.

We **BURIED**

There was a push toward you that happened naturally—
but there was dissonance, or more so the feeling that
we were over and misplaced, like wearing your prom
dress years later, the zipper snug on your skin, the cut
starkly outdated. Just as quickly as I pulled you out from
my bank of memories, you slipped back in. A couple of
blurry, black conversations and *I just don't want to be with
you; it's too much.* The cord of us and our high school
relationship tethered and ugly, now dragging out of sight.
Loneliness like quicksand surrounded and swallowed.

*I always hated that you wore a black shirt and a lavender tie to
prom. I thought it made you look middle-aged.*

We **SEETHED**

We said I love you in your driveway one evening in June. I was eighteen. Your head in my window, my cheeks on fire. I've never felt so mighty since then—not once. I've soaked you out throughout the years, and the pool once deep and blue and beautiful is now shallow and green and gross.

I had just finished a dance recital and told my mom that I was going to CVS to buy eyeliner.

I still smile at all of it.

I **BURNED**

Hello, I'm Betsey; ten dollars for ten minutes. This was a vice of mine—a few glasses of wine and I'd end up at the first psychic storefront I could find. I was greeted by Chico, a small white dog the whole room smelled like. He was prowling around in a purple turban, nearly knocking over the crystal ball covered in gold plastic leaves and the stack of sticky tarot cards. I sat on the folding chair. *OK, what do you see?* I knotted my fingers together as Chico licked my legs. *Your old lover knows you love him, and he loves you, but only through memories. Will we ever get back together? No, but I do see fortune. New lovers? No love. So what can I do? You're clearly very sexually blocked—your sex life is in shambles. For $75, I can light a healing candle and burn away the blockage. I don't have $75. What's $75 for a new sex life?*

I sometimes still wonder what that candle could do for me . . .

I **BLED**

I thought about you at night mostly. The days were
distracted with coffee chatter, subway lights, and splashes
of gossip and milling about the office. I thought about
your bear eyes, thin ankles, the Spanglish that would
make me laugh. I thought about the drum of your fan
and how you lied about Agnes sleeping on your couch
on Halloween. I thought about our hundreds of nights
in upstate New York in a wooden bed frame and how
those moments are threadbare and awkward to me now.
I thought about the times it felt cruel, the times you
would stomp and bite and hurl, bewilder me, belittle me,
the times on the gray carpet pleading, the times outside
the bar, the crippling lies drooled out, *I'll move to New
York, I promise,* dust balls of memory clogging my eyes
and my throat.

*And I would write your name in a blue notebook. Someone,
somewhere, would tell me this is the ritual.*

I **WAILED**

I careened toward human after human because the toddler in me just wanted to be scooped up from the ground and held.

Just as quickly as you're up, you're down.

I **DISPOSED**

I was in a strange place, shedding flakes and layers of old skin, of thick green nails, calloused and cutting. I was surprised to see my fleshy pink interior and how quickly it pussed and leaked on the floor of the downtown 1 train, on the blue plastic, on the faces of others. I would dress my pus in costume, gallivant under the river of the New York sky, slide into the silver steamboat of the subway, and emerge desperately at the surface, sputtering and slimy.

It was an undoing, a time of rewiring. It was truly the best of times and the worst of times.

We **FROZE**

You lived near Hudson Yards, which seemed to be fitting—
all of our interactions felt windy and slightly colder than
anticipated. We met at a birthday party. Your friend was my
friend, our names circling each other for years, yet there
was immediate distance. *Don't write a poem about me,*
you said, shielding your face with your hands. I laughed
and tried not to grimace. *What are you so afraid of?*
Because I don't like to be looked at or thought about like
that; I don't know—it's weird. And the truth is I found you
fascinating to look at—you were always on edge. I felt
like, if given the choice, you would unzip out of your skin.
We were incompatible in the most obvious ways; almost
everything I said made you wince, and almost everything
you said made me nervous. But here I am writing about
you—and see; it's not so bad. Someone looked and
someone thought, and nothing really came of it.

You acted like I was going to write a salacious article for the
New York Times. *Really, it was just a poem in the notes section of*
my phone. As Kate Winslet said in The Holiday, *square peg in a*
round hole.

I **INDULGED**

Talking to a psychic on the telephone, I sprawled at
the edge of my bed and stared out the window into the
next building. I'm not sure she's listening—*You have a
warrior's spirit and the grace of a deer. For five more
minutes, press pound. To connect to Edna, press 8.* I
closed my eyes shut and pressed 8.

*I just feel like deer are not all that graceful—especially suburban
ones that clunk and flail toward your car.*

I **ARRANGED**

There was a bed with blue sheets and a gray fleece
blanket, but now the mattress is bare. There was a cake
we baked together, and now the oven mitt is at my
grandmother's house. There was a dresser and a rug and
an orange helmet left behind at a storage unit. There was a
path of snow you used to shovel, but the snow melted into
water, and the shovel is in the shed. There was a pizza
dumpster in the parking lot, but now the lot is empty.

*I would often stare off into my thick silver computer monitor at
work and think of the dispersion of me and you and all our pieces.*

We **TUGGED**

I told you I wrote poems, and you asked to read one, so I
pulled one up on my phone. You placed a finger to your
lips and hummed, *Is this about Syria?* I laughed. *No, my
ex-boyfriend from high school.* You furrowed your brow
and ordered a beer. This divided us quickly—I was not
the politically charged Hinge poet you had decided I was,
and you were not the seamless first date I had decided
you were, assumptions packaged and sealed. You forged
forward—fingers wrapped around the red rose in a jar on
our table. *Flowers are just so totally beautiful. It's almost
too much beauty in one place, don't you think?* I think you
thought this might unite us. You licked your lips, and I
pressed mine together.

He was a TA/bartender with A LOT of opinions.

I **DETACHED**

I just did so much Adderall. It's 9am on a Saturday, and
I gawked at this text. *Why?* I wrote back to a boy I've
gone out with once. I turned over and watched *The O.C.,*
catching sight of my tired eyes in my laptop screen. *Just
in the mood to get fucked up today.* I felt starkly emotional
as Ryan drove through Chino, sunlight clutching his face,
Marissa crying into her large cell phone.

Where are you, Sandy Cohen? Come rescue me.

I **STIRRED**

Sunday is the loneliest day; that's why I spend it like an old Jewish grandmother, making soups and watching soap operas like my husband died, my children moved out, and I'm all that's left.

Meanwhile, all of NYC is holding hands at Westville.

I **TRUDGED**

Hours alone in the trenches of Bumble—Can I date
someone named Peep? Is he standing on the toilet? Why
is every picture with Grandma? Why does his bio say
"Obsessed with ham"—like the cold cut? Why are they
in a chicken costume in two of their photos—how often
are they in this costume? No to central New Jersey, no to
a selfie at their desk, no to cyclists (see PART I), no to the
word "cutie," "hun," "baby," "sexy," "sexual fantasy,"
"sexual position," "threesome," "ass," no to asking me
what I'm wearing, doing in bed, why haven't I found
someone. Hours and hours I spend with these creatures,
and to them I am a creature as well, and we are those
scaly, homely ghouls wandering around the internet
seeking a few glances, a few sparks down our spine.

It truly feels like a weird video game of avatars I get to choose from,
until I am walking into the bar and my avatar is awkwardly real.

I **CRADLED**

No one is going to take care of you like you took care of him, the thought bounces in my head as I slurred on the sidewalk in a disco costume. Loneliness drizzled through me coldly, greasy pizza oil covering my hands. *And they shouldn't,* I whispered to myself. *That's not what it's supposed to be.* I crawled into my bed and sunk into the wet wasteland of my brain.

The hardest person to avoid is yourself.

We **COMMENCED**

I can see the couple next to us watching our first date.
Oh, how sweet, they think. *We are old-timers. We have a
coffee pot and a welcome mat and a bed with blue sheets
that smell like us. We are on chapter 10 or 12 or 15. And
they are on page 1.*

*And they probably have a cat with an old man's name like Arthur
or Harold.*

You **UNLOADED**

We ordered lo mein and gyoza in a basement in
Chinatown. My first and last Tinder date. You rubbed your
chopsticks forlornly. *Are you OK?* I asked tentatively.
I'm sorry; I just . . . I lost my grandfather's jacket. What?
Your eyes were wet and round. *My grandfather died when
I was seventeen. I'm sorry. It was a dark time for me. That
was right before my dog, Melvy, got sick and the same
year Sara had the operation.* Pause. *And my mom moved
out.* The words poured like soy sauce down your chin. I
nodded sweetly, but by the end of the meal you were tired,
and I was drenched. We all need company sometimes. *Too
much?* I shook my head *no, no, no, no* and walked with
the hordes of families holding hands under big red lights.

Did you ever find the jacket?

I **BASKED**

Last October, we drove to West Texas with your dad.
He and I listened to hours of murder podcasts while you
slept. When you finally woke up, I reached my hand back
from the front seat, and you kissed my palm. Tonight,
I'm in a bar in New York having red wine alone, waiting
for a date, and it's on this night, this one small Friday
night, I have a few moments with you. No more than a
few moments until you are folded up and put back in the
dresser, back in the storage unit of my heart, sealed with a
big brass lock.

*I am downplaying the drive—it was SIX hours where you slept
and I chatted with your dad. Just one example of how I was a real
trooper.*

I **RENEWED**

We were supposed to meet months before we did, our story a setup with canceled dates, bad timing, curiosity, questions, a few late-night texts I entertained—a real saga that drew me in instantly. We finally met at a small, dark bar in the West Village, your eyes metallic and rolling over me. There was instant chatter, instant fissure. To make up sparks is easy, but to feel that guttural connection—it is always jarring and thrilling, like a revival. You worked in film, wore brown Chelsea boots, and had thick, sleepy eyelids. Hook, line, and sinker, I found myself in Brooklyn.

Of course, all trouble, but the very best kind.

I **GLEAMED**

In the root of the pit of my heart I exist in my rawest form—a homely middle-aged woman wrapped in fur, reading romance novels, and eating Cheetos. And sometimes on dates, especially ones that seem to be going well, I worry they can see the cheese dust glowing out of me.

Days of Our Lives *humming in the background* . . .

We **DIPPED**

We saw *Lady Bird* at a theater in Williamsburg. I couldn't
help it—I found myself crying throughout almost the
entire movie. Of course, you had every right to run out
of the theater alarmed, texting your friends about the
emotional train wreck I turned out to be, but instead you
offered your sleeve with a smile. *It's a lot like my mom
and me; we're very close.* We sat down at a dim, red
cocktail bar. *What about you and your mom? My mom
died when I was a teenager.* Then there was silence.
My impulse was to reach for your palm and say I was
sorry. This was our second date. I went with the impulse.
You lifted your hand from underneath jumpily and
summoned the waiter.

If only Greta Gerwig knew the drama she caused.

We **ROCKED**

You didn't like the restaurant I chose, the small Italian place in the Seaport. *Who comes this far downtown?* You chomped on your pesto. *I guess you do.* It was a year to the day of the breakup, my mind still pacing on the phone with a Texas landline. You never know what's swirling around in someone else's brain. I answered you quietly, *Next time we can go closer to you.*

The Seaport is so underrated—go to Il Brigante (side table to the right) on a February evening and you'll know what I mean.

I **THUDDED**

Sitting on the floor at a Christmas party in my best shirt, I
received the news about you from a third-party distributor.
He's not in Texas anymore, right? In grad school, right?
I swam into a big, wide, white pause. *And he's in
ANOTHER long-distance relationship; that must be wild
for you to see.* My entire body was hot pink and heavy. I
nodded and tried to keep my eyes from rolling to the back
of my head. *Yeah, wild.* I so wanted to flee the scene, to
zip up my parka and spill out in the elevator, but, instead,
I stood up, focused on the cheese platter, the salsa, the
sweet red napkins with Mrs. Claus. Later that night, I
walked with the yellow lights of the city and wrote you a
short little letter in my head, and I really hope, somehow,
some way, you got to read it.

*No matter who you are, hearing your ex has a new person is just a
big fat punch—it is a universal fuckery.*

I **EXPIRED**

It was a year of frosting and refrosting, but the cake was
rotted and brown.

And once you realize this, you can throw it away and begin again.

We **CLINKED**

Happy New Year! My drunk eyes timidly exclaimed at a crowded bar in Brooklyn, my 2018 sunglasses falling off my face. *You too! Let's go out for one more midnight drink?* And just like that, I was whisked into a new year, a new prism of excitement. These were the moments that felt surreal and thrilling. These were the moments that felt like a plot point—like the writhing was meant to lead me here to this one cab ride at 12:16 on January 1. There was something to be said for swallowing the tiny capsules of joy and letting them explode.

Hey, you might as well live up the new green sequined dress.

I **REVEALED**

Well, I'm all about personal sales. My company is a fucking joke—revenue is just not where it should be. But not me. I get after it. I was locked in silence watching your hands flail in joy at the mere mention of personal sales. I met you at a bar (albeit fairly wasted) a week before on New Year's Eve. *Sounds intense,* I offered, but I knew—I'm pretty sure you're not going to like me. *How are your personal sales? Why is the company doing so poorly?* I finagle the words around, stirring the red straw of my whiskey ginger ale. You were thrilled to get into it, and I gave it my all to listen. Two dates later, I mentioned I liked to write poems, and that was pretty much that.

I love the intensity of "a fucking joke." The passion that arises from selling insurance is truly invigorating for you.

I **SWELTERED**

Why is everyone engaged in Tribeca? I wondered at a
coffee shop on a Saturday afternoon. To my right, two
girls gushed over a princess cut, and to my left, a man's
shoulders were rubbed by a fat band of diamonds, the
sparkle side-eyeing me. I was in a black beanie and a
ratty sweater, appearing like the homely uncle that wasn't
meant to be invited to Christmas. My phone lit up. A
photo reminiscent of a mugshot has written to me on
Hinge—*Hey cutie. I could just eat you up.* But instead, I
ate a chocolate chip cookie the size of my face and tuned
into princess cut's decision of lilies over hydrangeas and
summer over spring.

Tribeca is for lovers (and old weird uncle types).

I **SMIRKED**

It was a basement bar in Brooklyn—the kind where time
feels elastic and neon signs are the only source of light. I
lingered my way around you and spoke closely. I was in
the mood to be on a mission. Your brown eyes flickered in
agreement. Sometimes, I feel like I am watching myself
from the ceiling with a bag of popcorn, shaking my head and
smiling at the boldness, the bright triumph of continuing.

*I couldn't tell you where or when this was exactly, but we all
collect nights like these, ones when we buck up and give it our all.*

We **TEXTED**

*Who is this? Hi sorry. Who is this? Met you a month
ago in Brooklyn through Hinge through John through
Cat through my coworker, your coffee was my coffee,
remember? My bad, sorry for texting. Hi there. Hey
you. Hey at 169 Bar. At that bar we went to last year,
the one with the popcorn, the one with the band, with
the big beers. I'm coming. I'm downstairs. I'm waiting
in the back. Why are you still single? Why are you not
answering? Where did you go? Where you off to? I'm the
one from Bumble from Hinge from your old job from your
friend of a friend's friend of a friend from Cat from John,
your beer was my beer, remember? It's been awhile. It's
been ages. Just wanted to be completely honest. Sorry
cutie. Sorry sorry. I feel terrible. I fell asleep. You're
really something.*

Hi, who is this?

We **BRUSHED**

I really love cheeseburgers and french fries. I love french fries too! You exclaimed so earnestly your eyes retracted in shame. It put me at ease. It was our first date in the East Village, a setup from a coworker—both cringing at ourselves, our islands of estrangement touching shores.

We are all so odd and sad on some base level.

I **REPLICATED**

There are four black tops, three pairs of jeans, and one
casual dress. I do the same wave in my hair, the same
dark-pink lips, the same black boots. There is such a ritual
of costume and performance—my script prepped and
read, my jokes timed with precision, the anecdotes I've
concocted about my family, my friends, my crazy boss,
my fake walls, my high school performance of Sandy in
Grease ready to go. It always goes the same—we saunter
onstage, our faces light up, we hug, we smile, we lean, we
scan each other for possibility, and then I go home, disrobe,
wipe off the paint, and fold myself back to the silence.

I can feel my brain mouthing along to the stories like a stage mom.

We **RICOCHETED**

On our second date, you told me you had been arrested.
I had just taken my very first bite of Bolognese at a
small bistro in Williamsburg. *In college, just got drunk
and did something stupid—really wasn't a big thing.* I
actively closed my mouth. I went to the bathroom and
googled you. "Disturbance of the peace during a hockey
game" was the caption of the photo I found—your mouth
open, eyes brazen, hands shaking a pillar at your college
stadium. I knew the photo would be plastered on every
corner of my brain's quiet village. I took my pasta home
in a doggie bag and flirted with the cab driver.

*The one time I avoided the normally obligatory pre-date google
since you were a mutual friend. Never again.*

We **RUNG**

I should probably tell you, though, I'm moving to LA. We met the old-fashioned way—at the bar counter, fighting to get a drink. It was Memorial Day weekend, and New York City was a wasteland of flowery spring air and garbage. It had been about three hours of syrupy banter. *You're moving to LA?* My eyebrows raised. *It's not a forever thing.* Your interest in me was refreshing. *What if we see each other when I come home for Christmas? And I'll be living in New York by next March.* When we said goodbye, our hug felt full. *I'm sold,* you said into my ear. I headed into a cab and watched you swim away from the window. I put an asterisk next to your name in my mind.

You were not my type—lanky athlete with a toothy grin who actually expressed blatant interest.

We **SPREAD**

You said I had an infectious personality. A large yellow
bulb went off in the hallway of my heart. I nearly cried on
the subway the next day realizing that after meeting me
once, you saw me the way I always wanted to be seen.

Severely hungover, my drama levels increase exponentially.

I **MEANDERED**

You should really meet my friend, banker, Upper West Side, CrossFit, German shepherd, 6'2"! . . . I stared at the photo of an overeager man in a tux tilting his head toward me, clutching a martini, rows of large teeth searing me like white glow sticks. I politely declined. I bought a soft pretzel and waded into the cotton June air alone.

It kills me when credentials are listed like ingredients—if only I could remove CrossFit, add a pinch of artsy and a dollop of funny, and replace the German shepherd with a Pomeranian.

We **ARCHIVED**

I really like your company, you said in the photo booth at the back of the bar—our eyes spotted with dots of white light. I kept the photo. It sits on top of my dresser, once loose, now hidden in the cover of a book about the subway system. There is an air about the photo that feels like we've been together for years in another life, in Cobble Hill with a fireplace and a welcome mat. But for now, we live on page 36 under the construction of the C train.

This was a date out of a rom-com, set up by our best friends, one I really bookmarked as one of the greats.

We **BREEZED**

On Saturday night, you sent me "Another Saturday Night"
by Sam Cooke, but I didn't see it until 4am Sunday
morning—and I played it, the raspy croon floating out of
my plexiglass wall and into the rest of the city.

There was something so old-timey about you, you felt made up.

I **ERODED**

I am so happy about this one, I admitted over chips and salsa with a friend. She nodded back. *You always say this though,* she said, not meaning to be cruel, but the words frayed my insides.

The language used when speaking to single people should be a course in college.

We **MOTIONED**

We mimic the movements of dating—the arm around my arm, the kiss on the cheek, my forehead, the hand on my knee, the fingers at the small of my back. I feel myself hatching into a strange, hairless being, never knowing that a moment of cluttering intimacy may be the last moment I ever see you.

It's one of the weirdest things to think about. Like, why are you tucking me in? You are three days away from ghosting me.

I **SUSPENDED**

There is no violent panic down the central nervous system
quite like *waiting for the text back.* Red sirens throb
below your skin—*False alarm! That was GRANDMA
asking if we got the birthday card* or *MOM reminding us
not to forget a scarf!* Or even worse—*That was Hinge—
Peep has commented on your photo.* Even when the text
arrives, you can't open it until you assemble the fire
department, the sheriff, the nurses from the CityMD
down the street, and, of course, Psychic Betsey—all
influential powers parked on the sofa as I unwrapped our
impending doom.

And as it turns out, you just hearted my last message.

We **SUBMERGED**

I've cheated on every person I've been with. I've never said that out loud. Tears drizzled down your face as you lowered your head onto my lap. *What?* This was our third time seeing each other. I found myself simultaneously cringing and wanting to comfort you—a maternal energy pulled my hand to your forehead. You were six years older than me, and you were crying in my lap. *I'm no good. You should know I've never been good.* How did I get here? *I've just started seeing a therapist; it's all so intense.* After that night, all the things came true that I thought might—I wouldn't hear from you, you would pick up a sweet, simple girlfriend to steer your road to recovery, and you would be distilled to the party anecdote my coupled friends shuddered at.

This was a date out of a rom-com, one I really bookmarked as one of the strangest. P.S. Same guy as the photo booth.

I **WAITED**

I find myself waiting for this seemingly inevitable you,
like the held breath of a countdown, like the footsteps
of the man delivering my pizza, like the zoom of my
family car pulling up my street. It is in this waiting that
I am simultaneously shrinking and billowing. It is in this
waiting that I just want to scream, *Come get me. I'm out
front. I'm in my party dress; you'll know it's me.*

Text me when you get here.

We **RIPPED**

On the beach late one night in July, perched on a lifeguard chair, beer breath and thick green waves, you leaned in, *I think there's still something here.* I wanted there to be something, anything, to make it seem fated and connected that my high school boyfriend was saying this, but the salty air wafted between us with no juice. Seven years of wear and tear, but, this time, the tear was too deep. I felt our old teen selves peering over in disbelief—the same pair, the same hands and eyes and lips, yet we had become so alien to each other.

Being drunk in your hometown always leads to something weird.

I **ILLUMINATED**

The only way I can describe falling in love for the first time is being told there is a light bulb—in the unfinished part of the basement, in the back near the Christmas decorations and the old mattress, and for years, you are certain there isn't. You're certain you'll always be fishing around in the darkness but still occasionally reaching for it, pulling at it, until finally, simply and sublimely, you find it—the light, the rich buttercream of a yellow light flooding the room, illuminating the green plastic tree and glass ornaments. Suddenly, there is so much to see. It is so starkly special, so starkly surreal.

And it really never lights up the same way again.

We **STEAMED**

Come back to my place in Murray Hill. Eyes blurred with vodka and the pink lights of the bar. At night, especially once it is almost 2am, my brain is muted and on autopilot and seeking warmth. You were sweating all over me, and I knew inherently how much I wouldn't like you at any other time; but 2am, nose to nose, the attention felt like hot sun on my back. *I can't do this.* I crawled home. I was lonely— so much so. It was on these nights it took all my might to remember there were expressways with signs, highways with gold lights, and side streets with diners and drug stores—there was a life beyond this rut of bleak August.

When you're in a funk, any semi-kept option in a fratty Meatpacking bar will do.

We **SCRUBBED**

I am very neat. I like order, you said, picking up your
martini and adjusting your royal-blue tie. I looked down
at the polish clawing off my toenails. I didn't belong at
a large, fancy Midtown steakhouse with a doctor. *I think
people who are messy just don't have their shit together.*
Sterile air wafts between us, and vodka singes my throat.

Once he called me "little lady," it was my cue to go.

I **CHAFED**

But I don't get it; why don't you like him? He went to Harvard! my friend asked me on a bench in Washington Square Park as I told her about a second date with a doctor from Hinge, July sizzling our shoulders. *Just feels weird,* I said, and she shook her head. *You're never going to find anyone if you're this tough.* I watched two dogs nip at each other's fur as my ice cream melted on my shirt.

He was pristine on paper—but total beige Natasha vibes (if you know, you know).

We **TEXTED**

You're really cute. You think so? You're really not going to answer? I'm struggling. Hungover, you? Been thinking—I know this is out of the blue. Had a fun time. Last night was great. Thanks so much. I know you just got out of something. I get it—wish you the best. Wish you were here. Wish you would come to Brooklyn, come by, come over, come here, go meet me there. How are you, anyway? You looked good. Not going to lie, you've been on my mind. Happy New Year. Happy birthday. Happy first day. How's your Sunday? How was last night? How's your Tuesday? Wednesdays are the worst, right? Thank god it's Friday. What's your plan? What's happening? What's up? What am I going to do with you?

How are you, anyway?

We **THRUSTED** (actually, we did not)

Camping out at Planet Fitness, I turned toward you sitting at the front desk, your purple polo a stark contrast to your scowl. *Can I help you with something?* You glared at my small silk dress. *I'm supposed to meet someone.* I pointed across the street. *Just kind of need a minute . . . just so tired of doing these things . . .* You turned to the computer. *Are we not in this together?* I pleaded in my head. *Look, you can stay here for a little, but then I'll need to ask you to leave.* Your tan muscles rippled under the purple; your underbite snarled. If this were a movie, I would have slowly walked over and whispered something cheesy and horrible, and we would've made out in your purple plastic chair. But this was not a movie; this was me getting kicked out of Planet Fitness in a small silk dress.

Your name tag said Titus, and I'm sorry, but I just don't believe that was your name.

I **COWERED**

You were wearing a tight corduroy blazer and clutching
wildflowers, both of which seemed bewilderingly formal
for a first Bumble date. I slowed my pace when I saw you
tapping your foot outside looking for me. I was in a small
silk dress. My stomach rolled. You were my strange,
secret Bumble pen pal—for months we chatted on and
off, and I daydreamed about you. But there you were—
shorter, wider, and weirder than the scruffy blue-eyed
headshot I was first drawn to. Of all the strange moments
I've had, this felt the most severe.

Aren't we all catfished at least once?

We **UNRAVELED**

One of the days just before graduation, we danced on the
turf field, and you said, *Forget about New York, forget
about Texas, let's pick somewhere and just go.* But I
wasn't going to forget about New York, and we weren't
the kind of couple that starts a life in New Mexico with
a houseplant and a tiny cottage near the market. We sent
a sweaty, happy photo to my parents, our faces stuck
together like thick paste.

*This tiny memory slinked into my mind as my coworker showed me
her family's new house in Albuquerque.*

We **HARDENED**

We haven't spoken in two years—a block of ice that I live comfortably next to.

Every so often, I let my fingertips graze the smooth, cold surface and watch it melt ever so slightly.

We **GUZZLED**

I convinced you to come to the psychic with me—the one on 23rd Street. I was in a phase where I was swiping erratically. We took tequila shots at the dive bar next door. The psychic was a petite woman with a large middle and big chandelier earrings. *This could be your soul mate,* she said to you, winking at me. I chuckled. Once I sat down, she shook her head. *Ah, but you, you have a lot of life to live; it's gonna be awhile.* We went back to the bar next door and pretended like that didn't happen.

I consider this a low point for all three of us.

I **DODGED**

Am I ever going to see you? you messaged me on
Instagram. I stared at the words, and I felt like a monster.
I'm so busy this week!!! It's a busy time for me—a cloud of
vagueness sifting between us. I minimized the conversation,
headed back out to the wilderness of my phone, and let
Mom know I did indeed get her birthday card.

*It was not a busy time for me. I spent that particular week
watching* The Real Housewives of NYC *from start to finish and
ordering tote bags on Etsy.*

I **WEIGHED**

I knew you liked me and I didn't like you, and this feeling
sat in my back like dumbbells. It was strange being on the
other end of things—the power not so thrilling to hold.

Sigh. Big, long, sheepish sigh.

I **RECEIVED** (advice)

Do you do the apps? You should try the apps. You should join something! Dodgeball? Running club? The gym? Maybe you should just go out, you know, be friendly, be chatty, be open. You have to put yourself out there. There is this place in Brooklyn, this park downtown, this small wine bar with twinkle lights, where everyone meets their husband at. Are you being weird on these dates? Don't be too loud, too busty, too chatty, too artsy, too sassy, too open, too confident, too drunk, too sweet, too animated. They will not take you seriously if you order a burger. They will not take you seriously if you wear that leopard coat, those boots, that blond hair. DO NOT mention your writing, so weird, wow. Why don't you flirt with the waiter? With your cousin's friend? With your coworker? Are you even trying? You didn't meet anyone at the party? There were so many boys! Were you being weird? Why don't you text him, go on, go text him, see what he's up to. Just don't be too much, they hate too much, oh you, you're definitely being too much.

And alas, I'm always too much.

I **CHILLED**

In Midtown, I swirled my red straw around a whiskey
ginger ale at the office Christmas party, the ice block of
December pressing down on me. I flirted with the kind
accountant in the midst of yellow paper lanterns from
Party City, wondering if anyone would text me *Merry
Christmas* this year.

*And Lydia shows me her podiatrist nephew in the hopes I might
take the bait.*

I **DECAYED**

I had a straight three weeks of dates—like a movie montage of a divorcée speed dating—*Hi! Hey yo! Yo. I'm the banker, the writer, the insurance guy, your typical New Jersey transplant, Morgan Goldman Stanley Sachs, banks, banks, my job is crazy, my job is harder than yours, my job, my job, my writing, my film, my dumb art, upper Chinatown, lower Bed Stuy, upper west corner of the Lower East Side, my mom's basement, friend's couch in Queens, sister loves horses, mom works in marketing, dad lives in Europe with his illicit secretary, my friend Ronnie is crazy, my friend Mike is the best, crazy enough, I love pizza, crazy enough, I love Bud Light, from the middle of New Jersey, California, Ohio, love football, soccer, really more of a baseball guy, love the Patriots but hate Brady, love the Rangers but hate the cold, you're really pretty, you know that? You're really cute, you know that? You're actually funny, you know that? Come back with me, no me, no me, no, you really won't come back with me? Why did you kiss me in the restaurant, then? Leading me on, yeah, you know it, you don't have to come back with me, FINE, next time, next time, you won't be this tough, next time, you know you will.*

And they whirl into one scruffy, blurry face with a long nose and a big mouth.

I **DULLED**

My heart became a numb tooth.

True loneliness isn't a feeling—it's the absence of it, the empty chair, two sets of chopsticks for an order of one.

We **GLINTED**

Happy New Year, I said, but it was still December. We were on the corner of the West Side Highway with your hands in my pockets. You were confident in the kind of way that is startling—a magnetism that glows. For the first time in a long time, I didn't want to leave. But you were—headed back to California in a few hours, our strangely sound dynamic to be put on hold again. *Someday, maybe,* I whispered lightly, and the bell of my stomach quaked.

And I reaffirmed the asterisk I placed next to your name all those months ago.

We **EXHALED**

You sent me a picture of the sunrise in California, and I saved it. *Good morning.* Sometimes I like to imagine us on the beach talking lightly, orange puckering through dark night, waves rocking like heavy breath, beach towels, warm air, leg over leg, eyes into eyes.

And I hear the Beach Boys playing, cheesy enough.

I **PLUNGED**

Wandering around the West Village waiting for a friend,
I walked with myself for a few blocks, the cool hands of
January on my chest. I sighed into the swell of solitude,
the quaint street, my brain delicately in conversation with
itself. I mustered the words I've finally strung together
after months of pretending—*I'm waiting for you to get
here, and you're not coming.* And it's not sadness but
loneliness that pours, fizzes through my head—another
bottle of hope emptied into the sink.

*But it's important to remember there are more bottles in the
basement.*

I **MUSED**

Sitting on a pile of clothes on the floor of my bedroom,
I am entrapped by my hut of plexiglass and plaster, the
murmur of my roommates and their boyfriends wafting
about. Sometimes I dream about living with someone,
shuffling past him in the kitchen with a bag of lettuce,
touching legs under clean gray bedding, watching TV
with the lights off and pajamas buttoned and soft. But for
now, I slide my barn door open and heat up my dinner.

And I'm sure someday I will long for my plexiglass cage.

You **SPOUTED**

You wanted to play the question game—the idea of
gamifying our first date made me cringe, but I smiled.
What's the weirdest place you've had sex? Before the
question left your lips, so did your response. *In the shower
in the middle of a family Christmas party with my ex,
Susan.* Your eyes darted with the slip of her name and
this strange admission. I felt it—the pulsing palpability
of Susan. I imagined thin, wiry legs, electric green eyes,
a laugh that echoed through the dark wood of the bar.
Haven't heard from her in a while. You trailed off, and
I meandered there with you. I was your *getting back out
there*—your shaven chin, your neat blue button-down. And
you were my umpteenth dating app date. Next question.

Why the shower? *I wanted to ask so badly, but I didn't.*

I **DUCKED**

Trader Joe's at 2pm on Sunday—I might as well have a
red neon light over my head: "SHOPPING FOR ONE."
Couples scurry like mice, squabbling over peas—*for that
pasta your mom makes,* over brown eggs—*no, no, we
never end up eating them,* over chocolate peanut butter
cups—*the wrappers end up everywhere,* over the two-
dollar candle at checkout—*come on, Michelle, we don't
need that,* and I bow my head and keep my hands tight on
the red cart.

And I always spring for the peanut butter cups and the candle.

We **TEXTED**

Just saw the subway poem—it's as great as you said. Just saw Cat, saw John, saw that coffee place, that taco bar in Brooklyn, just had yellow Gatorade—your favorite! Just heard that song, that movie, that word, that one and only thing we have to talk about at this point. Nothing. That sounds like fun. Not much here. That's so great! That's the best! That is my favorite! I'm at 169 Bar. At that bar we went to last year, the one with the popcorn, with the band, with the big beers. I know it's late, but are you awake? Are you coming? Come here, come by, go meet me there. I'll be early, I'll be there in five, in ten, so late, so sorry, why are you never on time? I know it's late, but look at the moon. I'm waiting at the bar. No rush.

Come here.

I **GRIMACED**

You're killing it—you responded to a photo of mine on
Instagram. What am I supposed to do with this? I sent a
screenshot to a friend and boarded the Q—romance like
a rat trampled under the tracks. *I feel like this is good,*
my friend wrote back—an Instagram response to a photo
where my legs look small and my face looks fake. A man
sitting across from me pulled out a banjo and started to
play Frank Sinatra. I closed my eyes to listen.

Do I write back, or do I just let it sit there, staring at me oddly?

We **REELED**

*I am working on this new project—it's about a superhero
fighting corporate America. You're writing a play?* I
responded, picking up a taco. It's our third date—Hinge,
handsome, slightly artsy, works in film, do we sense a
pattern? *I'm going to dress up in a Superman costume
in Union Square and approach your classic white man
in a suit.* The salsa was dripping everywhere. You were
losing me. *I want to inform them about evils of large
corporations, how they are warping our psyche and
fucking up our economy.* My brows folded together.
You're going to yell at random people? You knew it,
and I did too—you tried to roll the words back into
your mouth. *Yeah, I don't know. Just an idea. Yeah.*
We would see each other once or twice more, but
sometimes the ending is so loud, so finite, the closing
credits begin rolling before it all wraps up.

*You can bet I keep my eyes peeled for a red cape outside the 14th
Street Sephora.*

We **EVOLVED**

You were cooking chicken and brussels sprouts, and we were laughing like bright, bubbling teenagers—three hours with the lights on, New York to California, you talked me through each wall of your bedroom: a signed football, a picture of a sunset, white sheets, and bottles of sand. *I want to hear it all,* I said, and I felt your smile hot on the line.

I like to imagine you in an apron with a cheesy saying—don't be afraid to take whisks.

I **UNCORKED**

You were coming to New York for a week, which you said *just might have something to do with me*—I found myself counting down the days. I dug out the bottle of hope and set it out on the table.

Down into the basement I went.

We **PRETENDED**

I took you to my favorite Italian restaurant in the Seaport. *This place is so you,* you said kindly. We shared pesto and a side of meatballs, our eyes catching. *I just don't know when I'll be back; you know I could maybe move now, but I don't know, I love California.* You trailed off. You were the most I'd felt in a long time, so I tried not to listen, sauntering off with the Italian opera wafting above, grabbing for your hand.

I inherently knew all along it was never going to happen, but sometimes you just need a date with someone who isn't a total stranger.

I **CONSOLED**

The hardest ones are when I know you like me, but it's just not the kind that is enough. It is in these moments I go get a coffee, stare at the water, and sit with this body, this mouth, these parts I have learned not to blame.

I highly recommend Battery Park for such reflections—there are just enough happy couples lying in the grass to really amplify your loneliness.

I **UNEARTHED**

The night before Easter, I sprawled onto the floor of my childhood bedroom, unraveling the contents of a giant, pink plastic bin. I found myself digging and digesting movie tickets, a card with a lion on it, a paper crown, a snow globe, a pizza napkin saved from twelfth grade, a water bottle of sand, a sweatshirt, a pink cowboy hat, a bicycle magnet, mix CDs, a pen, and, of course, notebooks—some spiral, some diaries with ornate gold clasps, some tiny, some furry, some flowered, some empty, but all remnants in their own right, the notes and vows of my former life. And I remembered she's still alive; I'm still her. She just spends most of her time in plastic casing, preserved and romantic.

Who saves a napkin?

I **SWAM**

You wear that coat around? Not like a costume? It was
our first Hinge date slumped at the counter in the Lower
East Side. You were in a polo shirt with the name of your
college printed in the corner. *Not a fan of leopard?* My
vibrant grin fanned out—I was in the mood to persevere
and not to sink. You cupped your hand on your chin. *What
is it that you do again?* But before I could really explain,
you launched into it—*Well, I'm all about personal sales.
My company is a fucking joke—revenue is just not where
it should be. I get after it. What the fuck does that mean?*
I said, and this time I laughed.

"Must love leopard" is nonnegotiable—sue me.

I **CHOWED**

You sure can eat, you said laughing, your eyes marveling at me as I took a wide bite out of my cheeseburger. I ignored this observation and relished in my first and last free meal with you.

It's not J.G. Melon's fault you're an asshole.

I **LISTENED**

Walking through the city with my mother one Saturday,
she looked at me with warm hope. We stopped at a
Starbucks and huddled in the back. *Anyone on the
horizon?* I shook my head. I felt timid and sad looking at
her. *Just me.* We wandered around Battery Park. *I mean
look at Marcy's son; he met someone online, and they
couldn't be happier. And Jay met Mary at work, and they
are our favorite*—examples pulled from the couples filing
cabinet. I wanted to throw a tantrum, but I strode on.
Sometimes these people just fall from the sky, she said,
eyes bright and brown.

This is where my mother being always right feels important.

I **FLAILED**

What was I looking for? A few dates asked me this, and
I would tiptoe around the question, grabbing the waiter
for a drink, asking for a fry, shifting my silverware softly.
You're looking for a boyfriend! my friends would coo at
me, but the word "boyfriend" felt sterile and awkward and
somehow wrong. *For company?* I would ask myself, but
that made me feel like an eighty-year-old prowling around
the nursing home in hot-pink lipstick. And I think the
truth was I had no idea exactly what I was really looking
for and no idea what I was really doing.

*Though, I am excited for the older version myself in fur and a perm
flirting at bingo.*

Jenna Langbaum

I **STOWED**

I went on a trip to Austin to visit a friend who moved
there. I felt you in the long highway stretches, the melting
fudge at the gas station, the margarita breath, the whizz of
cyclists in bright orange. I kept this wrapped inside layers
of fabric—no need to wake the dead.

Texas and I have a complex relationship.

We **GRATED**

You sent a video of you and three girls drinking near a
pool in West Hollywood. I cringed. *Wish you were here,*
you wrote. I hate how much I replayed the video;
a strange concoction of jealousy, angst, and longing
coursed through me, lukewarm and awkward.
Have a fun night, I wrote back and turned on the TV.

It's these moments, I'm just like,
What the fuck are you doing, Jenna?

I **CONCLUDED**

I'm sorry; I'm not sure we should talk anymore.
You're not moving here; I'm certainly not going there.
I don't really see a point. I chugged cold white wine
and motioned the bartender. *Another wine, miss?*
The tangent of you grew tiring, and with a
few words, I packaged it up and began again.

Time to pull myself out of the cellar of denial.

I **ADMITTED**

I've realized it's not always them. As much as it's easier to place blame, it's not always the truth. Sometimes it's my fault. *Sometimes I just have to say I let the balloon go in the parking lot. It was me.*

A big red balloon sailing out of the CVS parking lot and into the sky.

Jenna Langbaum

We **CLASHED**

I'm a very serious person. My eyes narrowed. *Girls need serious, though.* I laughed. *Not this girl.*

And then he went on to say he fasts for twenty-two hours a day. I had so many more questions.

I **PLAYED**

It's hard not to think of dating apps like a game where eventually some outcome happens. If I am ghosted three more times, go on a Midtown sports bar date ten more times, stay positive six more times, be shocked to find they have a girlfriend one more time, and vouch to remain CALM AND CASUAL every time, then my prize should arrive at my doorstep. But the fact that there is no formula is what makes it simultaneously devastating and magical.

And to think my grandparents met in middle school and never looked back.

We **SPILLED**

You spilled your beer on the table and on my lap. You were a lanky cameraman in Converses. *It's OK!* I said, but I was cold, and the night felt long. *I'm so nervous; this is my first app date,* you said, tightly gripping the rag from the waiter. *It's OK,* I repeated quietly, even though I was too weathered and too tired to be your first app date.

And I paid for the drinks because you forgot your wallet.

I **SEALED**

Every so often, though it is very rare at this point, I wonder about you—and I always imagine a small apartment in Austin, even though I've been told you no longer live there, visiting your one-eyed dog in San Antonio on the weekends, driving on long stretches of Texas highway with music. I wonder what happens when you inevitably have a moment with me in your mind. I wonder how you categorized me in conversation, the words you shuffled through: "crazy," "emotional," "loud," "dramatic"— "dramatic" being your favorite. It's strange how it doesn't feel important anymore—any of it. It's strange how I ride the subway, walk home, fall asleep to different sounds and people, and you will never know any of it.

You have a sweet girlfriend now with a pool and a dog. And I'm almost sure you will marry her, and I will be your one strange, wild blip of blond hair and loud sounds.

We **SPAT**

Can I sleep on your couch? I'm actually between places right now. We met an hour ago on my friend's roof—our conversation fizzy and bright. *What?* I squint. *Why are you making this weird?* you exclaimed, irritated, the spring air suddenly spoiling. *You don't have to be a bitch about it. What? No, you may not sleep on my couch,* I said, slinking into a cab, sour and stupid.

"In between places" often lands you with the most dismal of recurring characters.

I **ASCENDED**

It was midnight in May in the back of a cab. The driver's eyes lingered in the mirror, and I felt him looking. *This is going to sound strange,* he said as the whir of the West Side Highway blurred beside me. *Oh lord, here we go. You have no reason to believe me . . . but I come from a line of African psychics*—my ears perked, and I started to laugh—*and I feel I need to tell you something: love is on the way. What? By July 15, you'll know who it is.* The driver's smile sparkled. *My name is Daniel.* He laughed, and I laughed. *I promise you.* I sauntered out of the cab and felt a silly sprout of hope poke from the soil.

And that is why I love New York City.

I **CHARGED**

Did you know Elvis Presley and the Statue of Liberty have the same face? I could tell this was one of your bits. You were sweaty. I imagined your cologne bottle was burgundy and situated under a large fraternity flag. *No, seriously, I mean it, google it!* You said "google" like a great-grandmother clutching an iPhone. I actively unpacked my level of desperation. I reached the point where being alone in air-conditioning and soft bedding was better than receiving a Bud Light and a spoon of attention from whoever would scoop it out. I googled it to be kind and strode away, Elvis's green face and black eyes judging me through the screen.

I admit it IS kind of crazy that they have the same face.

We **WALTZED**

We kissed at a tiki bar on the roof of a tall hotel, and it started raining. It was our first Bumble date on a night so hot the air hung like cotton candy. *You're sort of unlike anyone I've met,* you said with a trace of fear at revealing such a loaded line. I smiled widely, *I'm definitely my own gal,* hoping you would roll with me using a word like "gal." You did. And like so many of them, I left with a smile on my face and a goody bag of hope, tequila, and butterflies. But unlike so many of them, I felt a calmness the next morning. Maybe it was you, or maybe I was finally OK with not knowing.

The romance of July gets me every time.

I **OUTLIVED**

What I realized is that there shouldn't be curiosity anymore. I've had legs and mouths. I've writhed and wrung myself dry. But there is—and there will continue to be—the first brush of the knees, the first lamplight moment where redness pummels through cheeks and stomachs and all is forgiven and all is forgotten.

Short-term memory has fooled me once again.

We **PEERED**

On our third date, we took shots of Fireball at a dive bar, and you spun me around. We collapsed into a booth and tiptoed into the past. *I lived with my ex, actually,* you said casually, lightly, but the words felt grand and vast. *Oh, wow, OK.* The pause was static and filmy. *And what about you? Well, he lived in Texas, he did, he does, I actually don't know.* We pressed into the silence, the creak of our old lives like aching floorboards. But that was as far as we moved. We had more immediate concerns, like your favorite beer and the bartender's strange mustache.

And I bet you had a cat with an old man's name like Arthur or Harold.

I **GIGGLED**

Our fifth date was on July 15. We had burgers and large beers in Alphabet City. And all I wanted to tell you was that a psychic cab driver named Daniel said this might happen. But I figured if I wanted a sixth date, I probably shouldn't mention it.

Even my most cynical friends can't believe this.

We **PAUSED**

After one night when my text went unanswered, I was sure the ghosting would commence. I cocooned into myself and my bagel, anxiety throbbing like a fat pink boil on my face. *I don't think he's going to!* my friends said sweetly, as if not to probe the deranged, senile aunt. But I realized this time it felt worse, not so much because of the rejection but because I would have lost potential.

Hey! How's your Sunday?— and just like that, we are back in business.

We **SURPRISED**

You are a lawyer, handsome and tall, cerebral and warm.
All I can say is that there's a banner in my brain that
says, "Keep Going," and even though you're not what I
thought, and I'm very sure you think the same, side by
side, we feel like a set.

*I actually imagine you with someone waify, smart—a fellow lawyer
with thin glasses, shyly smiling at you in the conference room.*

We **LEVITATED**

Some phrases I've waited for. One in particular, the ultimate head-swirl heart-gallop heat-simmer-down-the-throat—*I'm not seeing anyone else; how could I?* You say it so quietly, so kindly, my eyes expand into white globes. But it's all in that late-night kind of way, when time is fluttery and things are so translucent they don't feel real.

I couldn't tell if I was allowed to bring this up the next morning; we still felt so breakable and new.

I **BIT**

It isn't easy—probing your numb tooth of a heart to
bite down again. There is such a lack of grace, a lack of
balance, a feverish need to protect and preserve the casing
of anesthesia. But there is also great relief in finally
feeling there is so much to chomp, so much to taste.

I think if you've read PARTS I and II, the clunkiness makes sense.

We **FORGED**

The milestones of the beginning are so specifically awkward—the first time we order food together, the first time you use my nickname, the first time you're sort of rude, the first time I'm sort of annoying, the first time my friend doesn't get your joke, I don't get your music, you don't get my clothes, the first time you really remember my family, the first time my skin on your skin isn't acknowledged or pulsing in intrigue, the first time I am actually me, no posing, no costumes, just bad lighting and crankier than you imagined.

The first time I hear my last name out loud from your mouth.

We **SKETCHED**

If you were an animal, you would be a ladybug. And you would be a lion. The Lion and the Ladybug. I like that. Like a children's book with a very sweet ending.

This is the kind of 2am conversation you have with someone new that you could never tell your friends about.

We **POPPED**

You smile at me sleepily, your eyes like tiny houses I wander through languidly. *Hi,* you say sweetly. We are in a cab on the FDR. And I feel it—the tiny red balloon in my rib cage breathes this new air and pops.

I'm sorry I gave you the ending. But I promise there's more to it.

ACKNOWLEDGMENTS

My first and foremost thank-you goes to Cynthia Manson, my insanely patient, unwaveringly wise, and undeniably insightful agent. Thank you for taking a chance on me; you've made my greatest dream come true. I love our long chats and our lockstep. I am seriously lucky.

This book would not have happened if not for the immense generosity of Andie Raynor—thank you for connecting me with Cynthia, a certainly life-changing email at that! Your kind, giving spirit propelled this book into a tangible thing, and I am so very grateful. Thank you to you and Cat for ferociously brainstorming, mulling, and sinking into this book at the final hour in the hopes of getting it published. Thank you, thank you, thank you; love you both.

Thank you to my editor, Patty Rice, for your sharp knowledge and faith in me. It has been the most wonderful thing to work with you and your team. Thank you for including me so seamlessly in every part of this exhilarating process. I still have to pinch myself every time I get an email from you!

To all the friends I sent this to, thank you so very much for your joy, excitement, and reactions. Thank you for jumping on the ride of all my crazy antics. (Special shout-out to Sam, who helped create the idea of the italics at the end of each piece.)

Last, but the most important, Mom, Dad, Al, and Ryan, thank you for your constant tidal wave of support and love for everything I do. Even though I know it takes up quite a lot of basement storage, you've kept my hundreds of notebooks because you've always believed! Without my gang, I would not have had the guts to do this! I love you so much; we're the best.

About the **AUTHOR**

Jenna Langbaum is a creative director, copywriter, poet, and playwright. Her original play, *The Night of Blue and Salt,* was produced in 2016 through the New York International Fringe Festival, during which she was declared by theasy.com as "a force to be reckoned with." Jenna grew up in Rye, New York, and attended Hamilton College, where she studied creative writing and theater. Jenna currently lives on the Upper West Side of Manhattan, fulfilling her lifelong dream of starring in a Nora Ephron movie.

Instagram: @jennalangbaum